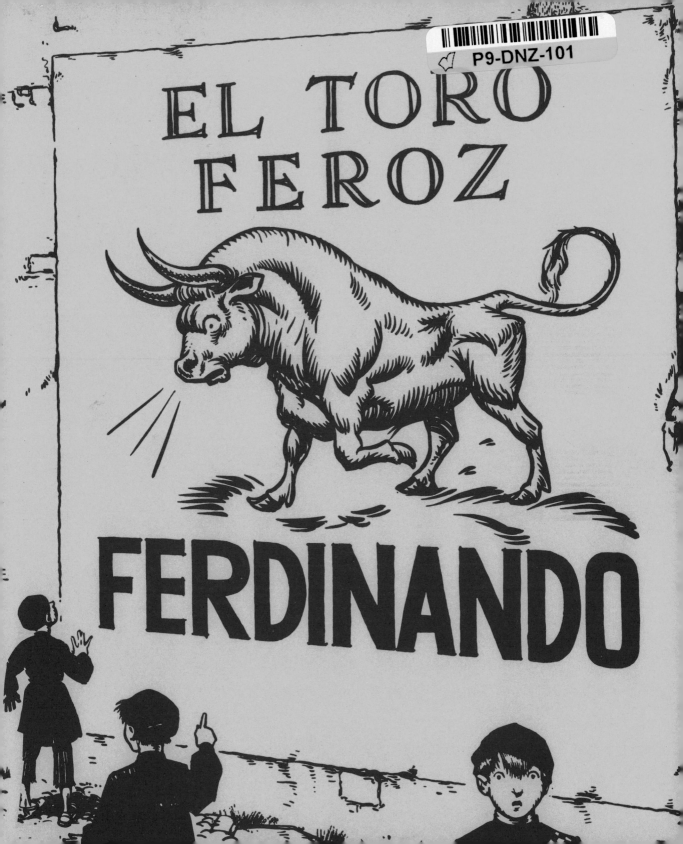

EL TORO FEROZ

FERDINANDO

The Story of
FERDINAND

The Story of
FERDINAND

By Munro Leaf

Illustrated by Robert Lawson

VIKING

VIKING

A Division of Penguin Books USA Inc., 375 Hudson Street, New York, New York 10014
Penguin Books Ltd, 27 Wrights Lane, London W8 5TZ (Publishing & Editorial), and
Harmondsworth, Middlesex, England (Distribution & Warehouse)
Penguin Books Australia Ltd, Ringwood, Victoria, Australia
Penguin Books Canada Limited, 10 Alcorn Avenue, Toronto, Ontario, Canada M4V 3B2
Penguin Books (N.Z.) Ltd, 182–190 Wairau Road, Auckland 10, New Zealand

First published in 1936 by The Viking Press
Published simultaneously in Canada
Library of Congress catalog card number: 36-19452
Pic Bk   ISBN 978-0-670-67424-4
Manufactured in China

93 94 95 96 97 98 99 100

Once upon a time in Spain

there was a little bull and his
name was Ferdinand.

All the other little bulls he lived with would run and jump and butt their heads together,

but not Ferdinand.

He liked to sit just quietly and smell the flowers.

He had a favorite spot out in
the pasture under a cork tree.

It was his favorite tree and he would sit in its shade all day and smell the flowers.

Sometimes his mother, who was a cow, would worry about him. She was afraid he would be lonesome all by himself.

"Why don't you run and play with the other little bulls and skip and butt your head?" she would say.

But Ferdinand would shake his head. "I like it better here where I can sit just quietly and smell the flowers."

His mother saw that he was not lonesome, and because she was an understanding mother, even though she was a cow, she let him just sit there and be happy.

As the years went by Ferdinand grew and grew until he was very big and strong.

FERDINAND
2 years

FERDINAND
1 year

3 MONTHS

1 week

RL

All the other bulls who had grown up with him in the same pasture would fight each other all day. They would butt each other and stick each other with their horns. What they wanted most of all was to be picked to fight at the bull fights in Madrid.

But not Ferdinand—he still liked to sit just quietly under the cork tree and smell the flowers.

One day five men came in very funny hats to pick the biggest, fastest, roughest bull to fight in the bull fights in Madrid.

All the other bulls ran around snorting and butting, leaping and jumping so the men would think that they were very very strong and fierce and pick them.

Ferdinand knew that they wouldn't pick him and he didn't care. So he went out to his favorite cork tree to sit down.

He didn't look where he was sitting and instead of sitting on the nice cool grass in the shade he sat on a bumble bee.

Well, if you were a bumble bee and a bull sat on you what would you do? You would sting him. And that is just what this bee did to Ferdinand.

Wow! Did it hurt! Ferdinand jumped up with a snort. He ran around puffing and snorting, butting and pawing the ground as if he were crazy.

The five men saw him and they all shouted with joy. Here was the largest and fiercest bull of all. Just the one for the bull fights in Madrid!

So they took him away for the
bull fight day in a cart.

What a day it was! Flags were
flying, bands were playing . . .

and all the lovely ladies had
flowers in their hair.

They had a parade into the bull ring.

First came the Banderilleros with long sharp pins with ribbons on them to stick in the bull and make him mad.

Next came the Picadores who rode skinny horses and they had long spears to stick in the bull and make him madder.

Then came the Matador, the proudest of all—he thought he was very handsome, and bowed to the ladies. He had a red cape and a sword and was supposed to stick the bull last of all.

Then came the bull, and you know who that was don't you?

—FERDINAND.

They called him Ferdinand
the Fierce and all the Banderilleros were afraid of him and
the Picadores were afraid of
him and the Matador was
scared stiff.

Ferdinand ran to the middle of the ring and everyone shout-ed and clapped because they thought he was going to fight fiercely and butt and snort and stick his horns around.

But not Ferdinand. When he got to the middle of the ring he saw the flowers in all the lovely ladies' hair and he just sat down quietly and smelled.

He wouldn't fight and be fierce no matter what they did. He just sat and smelled. And the Banderilleros were mad and the Picadores were madder and the Matador was so mad he cried because he couldn't show off with his cape and sword.

So they had to take Ferdinand home.

And for all I know he is sitting there still, under his favorite cork tree, smelling the flowers just quietly.

He is very happy.

THE END